When the Tide is Low

When the Tide is Low

Story by Sheila Cole
Pictures by Virginia Wright-Frierson

Lothrop, Lee & Shepard Books • New York

Printed in the United States of America.

First Edition   5 6 7 8 9 10

Library of Congress Cataloging in Publication Data

Cole, Sheila. When the tide is low.

  Summary: A little girl and her mother talk about all the things they will do at the beach, when the tide is low.

  1. Children's stories, American. [1. Tides—Fiction. 2. Beaches—Fiction]

I. Wright-Frierson, Virginia, ill. II. Title.

PZ7.C67353Wh   1985   [E]   84-10023

ISBN 0-688-04067-7   ISBN 0-688-04067-5 (lib. bdg.)

For Sasha—S.C.

For Janice and Allison,
in memory of Fred Toney—V.W.-F.

I looked out the window one fine summer day. Then I
said to my mother, "Please, may we go to the beach
today?"

"The tide is high right now," my mother said. "When the
tide is low, we will go."

So I waited inside and played with my toys. After a while
I asked my mother (in case she had forgotten), "Mother,
now can I go to the beach to play?"

And my mother answered, "Not yet."

So I said, "When, when can we go?"

"When the tide is low," my mother explained. "The tide is high right now."

"How high is high? How long will it be? Can we go anyhow?" I asked.

"So many questions," my mother said with a laugh. "When the tide is high, the ocean comes rushing over the beach and there is nothing but water to see."

"Where are the sand and the rocks where we play?"
I asked.

"Under the water," my mother told me.

"And the crabs and the clams that live in the sand and out on the rocks?" I went on.

"They are under the water now, too," my mother said.

So I went out to the yard and sat in the swing, and I rocked back and forth. (I was worried that there wouldn't be any beach for me.)

Then my mother came out to hang the wash on the line. "Mother," I asked, "has the beach gone away with the sand and the rocks and the crabs and the clams?"

"No," my mother said, coming over to me. "Once every day and once every night the water runs up on the shore and washes over the rocks and laps high on the sand." And she caught hold of the swing and pulled it back, back as high as could be, until it was over her head. "Then the tide is high, high like this," said my mother to me.

"Then, when the water is as high as can be, it starts going down, down, down, pulling back to the sea, like this." And what did she do, my mother, to me? She let go of the swing and she let go of me, so that I swung low, low, back down to the ground.

"Then the tide is low," my mother called out.

But before my feet touched the ground, I was floating back up, up into the air, swinging high as could be. "Now the tide is high again," called my mother to me.

"Oh, oh, it is getting low," I yelled, as I swung back down to the ground.

"So you see," said my mother to me, "first the tide rushes up high on the beach, and then it turns back and goes down. And if we wait until the tide is low, there will be all sorts of things to see."

"Will there be clams that close up with a squirt?" I asked.

"Yes," said my mother. "Where the stream empties into the sea." And she gave me a push so that I flew high. "Nearby will be the fiddler crabs with their claws held up like violins. When you try to catch them, they hide in the sand."

"Because they are very shy?" I guessed, as I swung back down.

"Because they are afraid that you'll eat them," my mother explained to me.

"Will we climb way out on the rocks?" I asked, flying by.

"Of course," my mother said. "That is where we find the shiny black mussels with long yellow beards, and where the purple stone crabs crawl on their stiff legs."

"I am going to catch them," I told my mother.

"They'll wave their claws at you," my mother warned me.

"I won't be scared," I said.

"We will look in the pools left behind by the tide," my mother promised me. "Sea anemones like little pink flowers live there."

"Can we pick them?" I asked.

"No. When you touch them, they close their tentacles into a tight fist, and you cannot pull them loose," my mother said, and she gave me a push that sent me back up, floating high over the ground.

"Then I'll catch the little fish that swim by," I called.

"They are small fry hiding from the bigger fish," my mother said, and she caught me in her arms as I came down. She nibbled my neck and gave me a squeeze, but I wriggled free.

"And I'll find a hermit crab," I told her.

"Walking by in his borrowed seashell," she said.

"And I'll find sea snails and starfish," I went on.

"But don't touch the sea urchins with their pointy spines," my mother warned.

"Will we watch a sea cucumber and a big octopus?" I asked.

"Not if we aren't ready when the tide is low," my mother said. Then she left me to swing by myself while she hung the rest of the wash on the line.

I went on swinging like the tide. Up, up, and then back down, down to the ground. I swung back and forth, up and down, high and low. But with no one to push, my swing slowed down, down, down, until I was just rocking there, back and forth, back and forth, like a boat on the sea.

And just as I was about to ask once more, what did my mother do but ask me, "Are you ready? Are you ready to gather some clams and chase the crabs and climb out on the rocks where the mussels grow? Do you want to touch the sea anemones and catch little fish and see all the things there are to see?

"Well then, come on, let's go. The tide is low."

GLOSSARY

Soft-Bodied Animals

A soft-bodied animal does not have a skeleton. The lower part of its soft body forms a muscular foot that the animal uses to dig or grasp with or to crawl on. The outer layer of its body, called the mantle, makes its shell or other hard parts. Clams, mussels, snails, octopuses, and squid are all soft-bodied creatures.

A **CLAM** has two hard shells that are hinged together on one side. It takes food in and squirts water out through its siphon, which it sticks out between its shells. Clams live in sand and where rivers and streams feed into the ocean. Clams are good to eat.

A **MUSSEL** has two hard shells that are hinged together on one side. Mussels live in groups attached to rocks and pilings between the high and low tide lines. They are good to eat.

An **OCTOPUS** has a beak in its mouth, like a parrot's, which it uses to tear apart crabs and other prey. This is its only hard part. Eight arms with suckers on them surround the mouth. To escape from its enemies, the octopus squirts ink and jet propels itself backward through the water. A shy creature, the octopus is usually the brown color of the rocks it hides under. It can be found in shallow water and near the low tide line. Some people like to eat them.

A **SEA SNAIL** has a spiral-shaped shell that it can pull its soft body back into. It moves with ripplelike motions on its muscular foot. There are many kinds of sea snails. Some are less than a quarter inch long, while others are up to twenty-four inches long. They can be found on rocky shores and on seaweed between the high and low tide lines, as well as deep in the ocean.

Jointed-Legged Animals

A jointed-legged animal has a hard, tough covering, called the exoskeleton, that protects its soft body. When a jointed-legged animal grows too big for this covering, it splits and the soft animal crawls out. A new exoskeleton soon hardens. The exoskeleton is jointed at the legs, allowing the animal to move. Shrimp, lobster, and crabs are all jointed-legged creatures.

A **CRAB** has five pairs of legs on which it scuttles sideways. Some kinds of crabs have pincers on the end of their first pair of legs. Crabs are found on rocky, sandy, or gravel shores and where streams and rivers feed into the ocean. The hermit crab lives in empty snail shells. Many varieties of crab are good to eat.

Stinging-Celled Animals

The round, tubelike bodies of these animals have a mouth surrounded by tentacles that are armed with microscopic capsules called nematocysts. Nematocysts shoot off like harpoons when the stinging-celled animal comes into contact with the animal's prey and paralyze it. Corals, jellyfish, and sea anemones are all stinging-celled animals.

A **SEA ANEMONE** has a mouth that looks like the center of a flower and gray-green, pink, or red tentacles like flower petals. If you touch a sea anemone, it pulls in its tentacles and mouth until all that is visible is a small circle with a slit. Some anemones bury themselves so that only their mouth and tentacles can be seen, while others live with their bodies exposed.

Spiny-Skinned Animals

A spiny-skinned animal has a hard skeleton covered by spiny skin. In some spiny-skinned creatures, the spines move, while in others they are fixed. All use their muscular tube feet to help them grasp food and move about. Sea cucumbers, starfish, urchins, and sand dollars are spiny-skinned creatures.

The **SEA CUCUMBER** is an oblong creature that has five rows of tube feet running from its head to its tail end. Its mouth is surrounded by tentacles. When a sea cucumber is disturbed, it spits out its insides. Different kinds of sea cucumbers can be found in reef beds or nestled among the rocks near the low tide line.

A **STARFISH** has five arms or more. On the underside, in the center of its flat body, is its mouth. Many kinds of starfish eat by pulling their stomach out through their mouth and placing it directly on their food. If a starfish loses an arm, it can grow another. Different kinds of starfish can be found on rocky and sandy shores, and on seaweed.

A **SEA URCHIN** has a dome-shaped body with a mouth in the center on its underside. The sea urchin's movable prickly spines can hurt if you step on them. Urchins live on rocky shores along the low tide line.

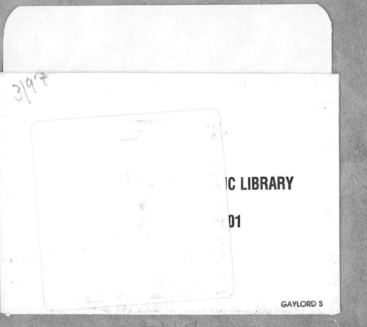